ELLIE

CURVY GIRLS CAN

SADIE KING

LET'S BE BESTIES!

Every week I send out an email with new releases, special deals and sneak peeks of what I'm working on. If you want to get on the list I'd love to meet you!

When you join you'll get access to all my bonus content which includes a free short and steamy romance in the Curvy Girls Can series.

Sign up here:
authorsadieking.com/bonus-scenes

ELLIE

CURVY GIRLS CAN BOOK FIVE

A steamy quick read instalove

Ellie

Only Brennan Jacobs could make me agree to a five-mile fun run. I've had a crush on him ever since I can remember.

But this body wasn't made to run. The training is grueling, the other runners are mean, and every time I see Brennan I'm hot and sweaty, and not in a good way.

But I'm determined to finish, no matter what the cost.

Brennan

I'm back from the military to take care of Mom, and I'm at a loose end. When I set up a charity fun run in Dad's memory, one of the perks is getting to spend time training with Ellie Smith.

She's smart, she's funny, and she may just be running away with my heart.

Ellie is part of the *Curvy Girls Can* series. Short, sweet and steamy instalove stories about women with big curves, big attitudes, and big dreams and the OTT possessive men who are man enough to love them. Each story comes with a guaranteed happily-ever-after, no cliffhangers, and all the feel-good vibes you love.

Curvy Girls Can is part of the *Maple Springs* world. A fictional small town where you'll find short and steamy romance stories.

Maple Springs series:
    Small Town Sisters
    Candy's Café
    All the Single Dads
    Men of Maple Mountain
    The Carter Family
    Curvy Girls Can
    Biker Brother's Curvy Christmas

ELLIE

’m wheezing as I climb the hill that leads to my house. It’s more of a slope really, but I’m so out of shape it feels like I’ve climbed Mt. Everest.

The mini-mart is only a half mile away, but next time I’m taking the car. This body wasn’t made to walk anywhere.

I’m just about at my house when a car cruises past and turns into the Jacobs’s driveway across the road. I squint at the figure in the front seat. Tall, cropped hair.

The man gets out of the car. He’s wearing tight jeans over a perfect ass and a fitted t-shirt that shows of the inked muscles of his arms, and even though he's not in uniform, you'd spot him as a military man a mile away. My mouth drops open.

Brennan Jacobs is back, and he's as hot as I remember.

Leaves crunch underfoot, and I jerk my head around just in time to bump my head against the maple tree on our front lawn.

"Watch where you're going," I mutter at the tree, hoping Brennan didn't notice. I glance across the road and he waves at me, which means he probably did see me walk into a tree. Great.

I give him a feeble wave back, and to my horror, he jogs across the road toward me.

"Hey Ellie. How are you?"

I'm red-faced from the hill, okay, the slope, and my t-shirt is stuck to my chest with sweat. If I was going to meet my teenage crush for the first time in ten years, I would have preferred to be wearing something less, um, sweaty that didn't cling to my belly.

But Brennan doesn't seem to notice and gives me a wide smile that seems genuine.

"I'm great. How are you?" I give him a big smile back, because he looks so damn good that I can't help but smile. Then I remember why he's back, and my face falls. "I'm so sorry about your dad."

His smile falters, and he looks down. "Thank you. After years of treatment, it was quite sudden in the end."

"I'm sorry you didn't make it back for the funeral."

He rubs his forehead and suddenly looks tired. "I was on a special operation, and by the time I was back, the funeral had happened."

A thrill run through me because it sounds so James Bond, but I try to act casual, like I'm not completely turned on by his military prowess. "It was a lovely send off."

He looks up at me, and damn, his eyes are the softest blue. "Thanks for going along. That means a lot."

I try to focus on what he's saying and not get lost in his eyes. "How's your mom?"

"She's fine, considering. She's had a long time to get used to the idea of life without Dad, but I don't think that makes it any easier."

"No, I don't suppose it does."

"How about you?" he asks, changing the subject. "I heard you were away at college."

My heart races at the fact that he's heard anything about me at all. But his mom is the biggest gossip in the neighborhood, so it's hardly surprising.

"I finished my last semester. I've moved back for a while to decide what the next step is."

"What did you study?"

I take a deep breath, ready for the ridicule that always follows my college major. "Art therapy."

He nods. "That sounds really interesting." I study his face for signs that he's making fun of me, but he seems genuine.

"Helping people heal through art. It works well on children." I say.

"Sounds like a noble thing to do."

No one's ever called me noble before, but I just shrug, playing it cool. "Seemed like a good outlet for my artwork."

The front door to his house opens, and Mrs. Jacobs wheels herself out of the doorway.

"Brennan!" she calls, then sees me and waves. "Oh, hi Ellie."

"Hi Mrs. Jacobs." I wave back and she frowns.

"Did you get the milk, Brennan?"

Brennan gives me a smile. "I better go and get the shopping inside for Mom."

"Bye," I say, watching his ass as he jogs across the road.

He gets to his driveway and turns back to me. "Nice to see you again, Ellie."

I go quickly into my house and shut the door. My heart's racing, and this time it has nothing to do with the steep slope I just climbed.

I've had a crush on Brennan Jacobs since I was eight years old and he stood up for me at the town fete when Carolyn Summers accused me of stealing cupcakes. Which I didn't do, by the way.

I mooned over him until he left for the military six years later. He was eighteen, and I was fourteen. I've seen him a handful of times since when he's been back on leave, but in the last few years, I've been away at college whenever he's been back.

I'm surprised he even remembers who I am.

I race up the stairs to my old room, where I've been staying for the last few months.

It's decorated as I left it before I went to college, pink with posters all over it. Mom hasn't had the heart to redecorate it.

I fall down on my bed and hug the pillow like I used to when I was fourteen. Brennan Jacobs is back, and I still have a massive crush on him.

2

BRENNAN

I plunk the shopping bags down on the kitchen bench, and Mom eyes me suspiciously.

"What were you talking to Ellie Smith for?"

What hot blooded man wouldn't want to talk to Ellie Smith? She's gorgeous and sexy with an innocent smile I'd like to kiss right off her mouth. But I don't say any of that to my mom.

"Because she's our neighbor. If I'm going to move back here, I need to be friendly with the neighbors."

Mom sniffs. "Her mom beat me in the church bake-off this year. I'm sure it was rigged."

I laugh. The rivalry between the Maple Springs Baptist Women's Prayer Groups is fierce, or it's all in mom's head. I've never been sure which.

"I'm serious, Brennan. Her husband made a large donation to the church, you know."

"You think he donated to the church so his wife would win the bake-off? Mom, that's ridiculous."

She gives me a knowing look and turns her chair around. There's a ramp that replaced the stairs into the living area, and she rolls down it. "You can't trust that family, Brennan."

I roll my eyes. Mom has a heart of gold, but she does like to gossip.

I put the shopping away, letting my mind wander to the gorgeous, sweaty Ellie Smith.

Her t-shirt clung to her body, accentuating her curves and showing off the two sweet mounds of her breasts. She certainly didn't have those when I went away ten years ago.

There's the sound of breaking crockery and a yelp from Mom.

"You okay?" I bound down the ramp.

There's an overturned coffee cup on the table, and Mom's holding her head in her hands. "I spilled my drink."

I put my arm around her shaking shoulders and rub her back.

"I'm sorry, Brennan," she says between sobs. "It just comes over me sometimes. I miss him so much."

My parents were married for thirty years. Theirs was a quiet kind of love, but no less fierce for it. They were utterly devoted to each other. The kind of love I hope to find one day, if I'm lucky.

"I know you do. It's only been a few weeks. It's going to take time." I put my hand over mom's and give it a squeeze.

"I don't know what I'm going to do without him." Uneasiness grips my chest. I've never seen Mom like this. She's never been helpless. Even after the multiple sclerosis confined her to a wheelchair, she's always been strong and determined.

"I'll be here, Mom, for as long as you need me."

"You can't just give up your career."

We've been through this before. With dad gone, I'm the man of the house now and that means taking care of my family. "I've applied for special discharge. I'd rather be here taking care of you."

"What will you do for work?"

There's a new veterans' center not too far from here in the mountains near Maple Falls. I might be able to find work there but I don't want to tell mom yet in case nothing comes of it.

"I'll think of something, Mom. Don't worry about that now."

Mom likes to be independent, but the truth is she

just can't take care of herself and my little brother. With Dad gone, it's up to me to take care of them. I've given the army ten years. I'm happy to do my duty by my family now.

I hand Mom a tissue. "I've had an idea to raise money for the Prostate Cancer Foundation."

Mom wipes her eyes. "Oh yeah?"

"I thought we could do a charity run. Dad was popular in town. I'm sure we'd get a lot of people taking part."

Her eyes are red, but they have some of her old fire back. "That's a great idea, honey."

"The money could help with research and maybe save lives one day."

She's excited now, and we make plans for the race while I clean up the spilled coffee.

It's not until I'm in bed later that I let my mind wander back to Ellie and those delicious curves...

3

ELLIE

It's a few mornings later, and I'm in my robe and slippers, yawning as I amble down the driveway. It's some god-awful early hour, and the only reason I'm out this early is to get the paper out of the mailbox for dad.

My mouth stops mid yawn as I spy an athletic figure jogging down the road. It's Brennan. Of course it is. Who else would be out jogging at this time of the morning? Only he's not jogging; he's stopping at every mailbox to post something.

Why am I always looking my worst whenever I run into him?

I turn on my heel and retreat to the house as fast as my slipper-clad feet will carry me.

"Ellie!"

I turn around slowly, tucking my robe around myself. "Morning!" I say, with a cheerfulness I don't feel.

He looks spectacular in his casual sweatpants that hug his thighs. He's wearing a hoodie that's zipped up against the morning chill, the zip straining over his muscular chest.

"I'm organizing a fun run to raise money for the Prostate Cancer Foundation."

He holds out a flyer from a stack he's carrying. I take one, and my hand briefly grazes his. Despite the cold of the morning, a warm current runs up my arm.

"Five mile fun run," I read, "Doesn't sound very fun to me."

He grins his easy grin. "You should give it a chance."

"What me? No way. I don't think I could walk five miles."

He laughs, making his eyes sparkle. "You always were funny, even when you were a kid."

I laugh with him, because I don't want to tell him it wasn't a joke.

I hand Brennan back the flyer. "I'll sponsor you and cheer from the sidelines."

He shakes his head and holds his hands up,

refusing to take the flyer back. "Not good enough. I want everyone in town with a pulse to take part."

The fact Brenna thinks I could run that far makes me wonder if I could. "I've never done anything like this before."

"Great opportunity to challenge yourself."

His eyes are dancing and my heart is racing, and who can say no to that grin? Besides, I spent last night at a meeting of the Maple Springs Businesswomen's Network. One of my old friend's Layla set it up and I've been going along since I got back to town. The women are inspiring and so far I've sat and listened and observed, wondering if I'll ever do anything as half as inspiring as what they're doing. Maybe now's my chance. "Sure. I'll do it," I squeak.

"Great." His smile widens, and I'm so happy I've made him happy that I grin back at him before remembering what I've just agreed to.

"You'll need to register online. Details are on the flyer."

I nod, the smile stuck on my face, because I've just agreed to run five miles, and the enormity of that is just sinking in.

"I'm doing a running club three times a week to train if you want to join."

"I have to train for it too?" I'm starting to break out in a cold sweat.

He gives me a quizzical look. "Of course you do."

I nod. "Yeah, of course."

His face turns serious. "It's okay if you've never done an event like this before. It's not a competition. It's about taking part. You can walk the whole way if you like."

I nod again, because I can't even walk five miles!

"You should come along to the running club. There'll be plenty of beginners."

"Yeah, okay. Sounds good." My head's nodding so hard I'm going to have a sore neck.

"I better go and post the rest of these. Thanks for signing up, Ellie. I really appreciate it."

I watch him jog to the next mailbox, wondering what the hell I've just signed up for.

It's the next evening, and I'm wearing the first pair of exercise sweatpants I've owned since high school. They cling to my thighs, and I keep pulling down my old t-shirt to hide the bulges.

There's already a group of ten or so people gathered when I get to the entrance of Winston Park.

"Is this the running group?" I ask a white-haired man who looks older than my grandpop.

"Sure is," he says, stretching a spindly leg out behind him and leaning forward in a lunge that makes his tiny shorts ride up his inner thighs.

A few other people are warming up, and I spread my legs and lean to the side, copying a limber woman up front who seems to know what she's doing.

A familiar-looking woman joins the group. She's wearing tight lycra that accentuates her toned legs. Her hair is tied back in a tight ponytail that swings down her back, and she's pushing a stroller with a sleeping baby in it.

She's swamped by half the women cooing over the baby. I want to go and look. Who doesn't love a chubby baby? But the woman is Carolyn Summers, or I guess not Summers anymore, judging by the enormous diamond on her ring finger.

Carolyn and her crew used to hassle the shit out of me in every gym class in high school. I was always the tubby, uncoordinated girl, the one who couldn't catch or hit anything.

I used to hate gym class. It was a relief when I could give it up and just do art. I couldn't hit a ball, but I could paint.

She looks as slim and perky as she did in high school, even after having a baby. I pull my t-shirt down over my belly and change my weight to the other leg. I lean far over my foot, hoping she doesn't see me.

"Is that Ellie Smith?"

Damn. "Hi Carolyn." I give her my best fake smile.

"I didn't know you were back in town."

"I've been back since college finished."

She looks me up and down and frowns. "You're not here for running club are you?"

"Of course I am," I say, with a confidence I don't feel.

Her eyebrows pull together. "I suppose it's a kind gesture. So sad what happened to Mr. Jacobs."

At that moment Brennan jogs up, already looking fit and limber.

"Thanks for coming, everyone."

Carolyn's head spins around so quickly I'm surprised she doesn't get whiplash.

"Hi Brennan." She gives him a flirty wave.

He ignores her and keeps talking to the group. "Today we're going do an easy two mile circuit around the neighborhood."

My stomach clenches because "easy" and "two miles" don't seem to belong in the same sentence.

"If you're a beginner, I want you to alternate between walking and running. Those who are more advanced can go around twice. It can help if you pair up with someone at your level. Okay, let's go.

I smile at the old man, thinking he might be a good running partner, but he takes off on his spindly legs and has soon disappeared with the front of the group.

Carolyn's out in front too, pushing the buggy with her long thin arms.

Brennan jogs on the spot, giving words of encouragement to everyone as they start off. It's not till I pass him that he starts to move, and I realize he's been waiting for me.

"Glad you made it." He flashes me his easy grin, and my tummy does a little flip. "I'll run with you."

"You really don't need to. I'll be slow." I'm already struggling to keep up with his slow jog. We've only gone a few feet, and I'm in danger of wheezing unattractively.

He settles in beside me, and our arms brush as other joggers run past us.

"How long are you in town?" I ask, hoping he'll

talk so I won't have to. I don't think I can talk and breathe at the same time.

"I'm back for good."

I almost trip over my feet. "Really? How about the army?"

He looks away and doesn't answer for a while. "That part of my life is closed. Mom needs me now, and Callum."

Callum is his little brother; there's a big age difference between them and he's still finishing up high school. "That's really good of you."

He shrugs. "Family first."

We jog in silence for a while as I muse on the type of man who gives up his exciting military career to come home and take care of his disabled mother and little brother.

The kind of man I could fall in love with, my heart whispers. Then I push the thought away, because that kind of man would never be interested in me.

"Your mom seems pretty good at taking care of herself."

"She's okay with most things. But with Callum still at school, she needs some help. I'd rather be here with them. Family looks after family, right?"

I nod, but it's getting hard to breathe, and there's

a burn spreading up my thighs. Brennan hasn't even broken a sweat.

"I have to walk for a while," I puff.

"No problem." He stops with me and waits while I catch my breath. "You should alternate walking and running when you start training. The important thing is to keep going."

"You should go on ahead," I say, indicating the rest of the group disappearing into the distance. "While you can still catch up."

"I'm happy to walk with you."

"That's kind of you, but no. You're leading this group. I'm sure there are others who need encouragement too."

He frowns. "You're right. You sure that's okay?"

"Of course it is. I'm not the only one in the group."

"No, but you're the best looking one." My mouth drops open, and he gives me a mischievous grin as he jogs backwards for a few steps. Then he turns around, and I watch his muscular legs stride easily to catch up with the other stragglers in the group.

I can hardly breathe, and it's not just because I've been jogging; Brennan Jacobs thinks I'm good-looking!

4

BRENNAN

I lean against the railings of the park entrance and watch the figure jogging slowly toward me.

Ellie Smith. Who would have thought the plain girl I played with as a kid would blossom into such a beautiful woman? In her tight sweatpants and baggy t-shirt, I can make out the curvy figure underneath.

But there's something about her, her natural smile and the way she makes me laugh. She's beautiful from the inside, and it shines all the way through.

As she gets closer, I can see the determination on her face. It's three weeks into the training, and she's pushed herself harder than anyone else in the group. She sees me waiting for her and that smile spreads right across her face, lighting up her eyes and shooting me straight in the heart.

I hold my hand up, and she high fives me as she reaches the end of the circuit. She comes to a stop and bends over, her hands on her thighs, gasping for breath. I have a sudden vision of Ellie on her hands and knees, gasping as I ram my cock into her.

I shake the vision out of my head, but not before my dick responds and I have to bend over to hide my hard-on.

"First time I've jogged all the way around," she says between gasps. "Two miles. I just ran two miles." She pumps her arms in the air, and she's so pleased with herself that it's infectious.

"Almost halfway there."

Her smile falters. "Not even halfway. My calves are tight, and my thighs are burning.

I try not to think about her luscious thighs. Luckily, she keeps talking while I adjust my pants.

"I can't even imagine going around again."

"Come back to my place. I've got something that'll sort you right out."

She raises her eyebrows. "What's that? Secret military sauce?"

I laugh. "Something like that. Protein shake."

She screws up her nose. "Won't that make me grow testicles?"

I snort laugh. "I hope not."

We head back to my house, chatting easily. Something about Ellie puts me at ease, and I find myself able to talk to her about anything.

We walk up the ramp to my place, and I hustle her into the kitchen. I grab the blender, some frozen fruit, and a couple of scoops of chocolate-flavored protein powder.

"And now for my secret ingredient." I take out the jar of peanut butter and add a generous spoonful.

Her eyes light up. "I know already I'm going to love this."

I blend it up and pour out two glasses. We clink them together, and I watch her closely as she takes a sip.

Her eyes roll backwards, and she makes a sexy "mmmm" sound that makes my dick twitch. "That is delicious."

I can't help grinning.

She takes another long sip and nods her head slowly. "If I'd known about these, I would have taken up exercise years ago."

"I always have one after a run or a workout. Helps repair muscles so you don't get achy."

"I usually just go home and have a long soak in the bath."

And now I'm trying not to think about Ellie naked in the bath. Damn. She's leaning against my kitchen counter. Her t-shirt is damp with sweat and clinging to her boobs, and she's got a chocolate mustache from the shake. She has no idea how gorgeous she looks right now.

"You've got chocolate on your lips."

Her tongue darts out and laps at the chocolate. "Did I get it?"

"Almost." My voice is husky, and I take a step toward her so our bodies brush. She's looking at me expectantly, and I have a bolt of realization. She wants this too.

I close the distance between us, and my mouth crashes into hers. She kisses me back, and I taste chocolate and her sweet salty sweat. My tongue darts into her mouth, and I roll it under her teeth.

My body presses against hers, my dick hardening at the sensation of her soft body. I slide my hand around her waist, and it feels so good to hold her. Her lips are soft and sweet, and I lose myself in the kiss.

There's a banging noise behind me, and we jump apart.

Mom is clumsily wheeling herself up the ramp into the kitchen, her foot hitting the side of the wall in such a way as to make a lot of noise and let me know for sure that she saw what was going on.

I start to go red, and then I remember I'm not a teenage boy being caught making out by his mom. I'm a grown-ass man being caught making out by his mom. So I lean causally on the counter and finish my shake.

"Hello Ellie, dear. How's the running?"

Ellie is bright red, but she gives Mom a big smile. "Good, yeah. I did two miles without stopping today."

"Good for you. Race is only two weeks away though. Still a long way to go."

Ellie's face falls, and I shoot Mom a look that says she could try to be nicer.

"Ellie's doing great," I say, "and you don't have to run all the way around. Walking is just as good."

"Yeah, I know," says Ellie. "But now that I've signed up, I want to run it all."

"Better get a move on then, dear. Unless your mom has a plan to drive you half the way, drop you off, and make it seem like you ran."

Ellie shoots me a confused look. And I gape at

Mom, but she's pointedly looking away pretending she didn't just throw shade at Ellie's mom.

"Um, I better get going," says Ellie awkwardly.

"I'll walk you home."

Mom gives a shrill laugh. "She only lives across the road, Brennan."

So now I've got my mom cock blocking me.

"She's right," says Ellie. "I'm gonna go. Thanks for the shake."

Before I can stop her, she's out the door.

I don't get a chance to check that she's okay or to say that it wasn't just a kiss, that I've been imagining kissing her ever since I came back here. I don't get to tell her that it could be the start of something. Because already I'm getting all the feels for Ellie Smith.

5

ELLIE

It's been seven days since I kissed Brennan Jacobs, and a tingling sensation tickles my lips whenever I think about it.

There have been two more running clubs, and we've fallen into an easy routine. He runs with me for about the first mile, and then he goes ahead to support some of the other runners. I'm always at the back, so he makes his way through, easily catching up to the next slowest and giving them words of encouragement before moving ahead to the next.

He waits for me at the end, and we walk home together. But his mom is always there with some errand or other for him to do, so there've been no more kisses.

I've wondered why he doesn't ask me out, but I guess he's busy organizing the race and looking after his mom and brother.

I'm doing my warmup stretches at the park, looking anxiously at the sky.

"Could be a wet one tonight," says Karl, the old dude. He's wrapped up in a parka pulled tight around his face.

I glance around and just about everyone has some kind of wet weather covering except me.

"I'll just have to get wet then." I give him a bright smile.

"Be careful. Road can get slippery in the rain."

He gives me a nod and heads up front to join the fast runners. I've gotten to know most of the people in the group over the last few weeks, and they're a good bunch. Well, most of them.

My eyes narrow as Carolyn jogs up to the group, her ponytail bouncing. She flashes Brennan a smile of perfect teeth.

"I managed to get away without the baby tonight." She touches his arm, and my stomach goes tight. Is she flirting with him? Her finger twirls a strand of her hair. Oh yeah, she's flirting with him all right. "I thought we could run together. I'm faster without the stroller."

He glances back at me and I look away quickly, hoping he didn't see me gawking at them.

"I always run the first mile with Ellie," I hear him say, to my relief.

"That must be hard," says Carolyn. "To go so slowly. You must be dying to actually run."

My cheeks are burning up, and I bend down to tie my shoelace, which doesn't need tying.

"It's my favorite part of the run," he says.

The knot in my stomach loosens, and I smile to myself. I stand up again, and he catches my eye and smiles.

Carolyn flips me a dirty look and slinks off to join her friends. She's dragged some of the other mean girls from high school to the running club. She whispers something to them, and they glance over at me and giggle. And suddenly I'm transported back to high school gym class.

Carolyn and her best friend are picking teams for volleyball, and I'm the last person left. The teacher is talking to a messenger who's come in from the hall, so she doesn't see that they're doing rock, paper, scissors and whoever loses has to have me.

Half the class is giggling and half the class is telling them to stop being mean, but it doesn't stop

Carolyn's look of disgust when she draws rock to the other girl's paper and loses.

I stand for a moment, hoping the floor will swallow me up. The gym teacher breezes over.

"Have you chosen teams?"

Everyone's silent for a moment, waiting for someone to tell her what just happened. But no one does, not even me. With my head down, I shuffle over to join Carolyn's team.

I'm jolted back to the present by the rush of runners around me. Karl slaps me on the back as he goes past. "Good running tonight."

I mumble something after him and make myself move, even though my feet feel heavy as lead.

"You okay?" says Brennan, looking at me with concern.

"Yeah, just feeling tired tonight."

"Push through it, girl. You know you can do this."

Usually his cheerleader act really helps, but tonight my feet are stumbling and there's a heaviness in my heart.

"Maybe you should go on ahead tonight."

He frowns at me. "No way. You're stuck with me for at least the first mile."

His grin improves my mood, and as he starts to chat about his day I feel myself relax.

"Did you know your mom stopped by today?" he asks.

"What, to visit your mom? I thought they were sworn enemies."

"From what I can gather, they're frenemies. She brought her some homemade strawberry tarts."

"That's Mom's best recipe. She must really want to make amends."

"It must have worked, because they sat cackling in the living room for about an hour."

I can't help but chuckle. "Gossiping about the neighbors no doubt."

"Oh for sure. But after she left, Mom asked me how you were doing with the running."

I laugh. "So Mom's strawberry tarts really sweetened her up, huh?"

"Seems like it."

We both laugh, but I'm getting out of breath, so I tell him to go on ahead.

The next slowest is a middle-aged couple, Gary and Linda, and he heads off to catch them up and run a bit with them.

It's coming up to the second mile when the first rain drops land on my skin. They start big and thick, and at first the coolness is nice against my hot skin.

I keep going in the rain for a while, not minding the drops on my heated skin.

After a while it starts to get a bit slippery, and I search for somewhere to wait it out.

I come to a street lined with maple trees, and I can see some of the other runners sheltering under the first big tree. Just as I reach the trees the rain comes down harder, and I push myself to get under cover before I'm totally soaked.

It's Carolyn, and she's holding court with some of the other runners. She looks totally dry, like she must have been sheltering since the rain began.

They don't see me, which is fine because I'm hunched over catching my breath.

"He is so inspirational," says Carolyn. "Doing all this for charity."

I smile to myself, realizing they're talking about Brennan.

"The way he encourages people is amazing," she says. "Practically walking that first mile with Ellie Elephant. What a saint."

I freeze at the use of the high school nickname that I haven't heard in years. Carolyn keeps going.

"He must feel the ground shake running next to her. I mean come on, if you're that size should you really be running?"

There are shocked giggles from a few of the runners, and at least some of them have the decency to look awkward.

One of the group spots me and gives Carolyn a pointed look. She turns around, and I pretend I've just arrived under the tree.

"It's gotten wet out there," I say, shaking rain off my t-shirt. My cheeks are burning, but I'm flushed from running anyway.

"Hi Ellie," Carolyn says sweetly. "Looks like you got caught in it."

"Yeah, it's really coming down."

"We were just about to start out again." She looks around at the group, and there are relived nods all around.

I peer out at the rain. "I'm gonna shelter here for a while."

"Suit yourself."

They head out into the rain, and I watch them go. My stomach is tight with hurt and anger. Anger at myself that even after all these years, I still didn't stand up for myself.

Carolyn's right: I'm not made to run. It was stupid to think I could do five miles. And Brennan only talks to me because he feels sorry for me.

How pathetic I must appear to him with my face

bright red, in my old t-shirt and sweatpants, barely going faster than a walk. He kissed me once and realized it was a mistake, which is why he's never tried it again.

I wait until they're out of sight, and then I break cover, but instead of continuing on the jogging route, I turn the other way and head home.

6

BRENNAN

Early morning birdsong greets me as I head out the front door. I glance up at the clear blue sky. It's race day, and it looks like it's going to be a beautiful day, but there's an uneasy feeling in my stomach as I cross the road.

Ellie hasn't been to any of the running sessions this week, and she hasn't returned my texts. I should have stopped by sooner, but I've been busy with the event, dealing with last-minute entries and setting up the course.

It loops around town and finishes in the park. We've had over 2000 entries and so far raised over $50,000 dollars. I should be smiling, but there's a frown on my face as I bang on number 22.

Ellie's mom opens the door in her robe and house shoes.

"Oh, hi Brennan."

"Sorry to disturb you so early, Mrs. Smith. Is Ellie home?"

"She's still in bed, but come on in. I'll see if she's awake."

I follow her into the kitchen and wait while she climbs the stairs. I glance at my watch. She's cutting it a bit close, still in bed when the race starts in an hour.

I hear someone coming down the stairs and a minute later, Ellie comes into the kitchen. Her hair is a mess, and she's wearing stripy pajamas. She rubs her eyes like she's just woken up. She looks warm and adorable, and I just want to give her a big hug.

"Do you want a lift to the race today?"

She gives a big yawn and shakes her head. "I'm not going."

"What?" My mouth drops open and a gape at her.

She crosses the kitchen and fills the kettle at the sink. "You want a coffee?"

"After all your hard work?" She's come so far; I can't believe she'd give it all up like that.

"Don't look at me like that," she says, switching

the kettle on. "I tried. I'm not a natural runner. I'm not going to be able to finish it, so what's the point?"

I study her for a moment. She looks weary, distrustful. "Something happened, didn't it?"

"No." She turns away to get mugs out of the cupboard.

"Did someone say something?"

She shakes her head. "It's nothing. Just dumb high school stuff."

I must be missing something. "Uh, didn't you finish high school quite a few years ago?"

"Yeah I did, but it seems some people are stuck there. That's why I'm leaving town."

The bottom falls out of my stomach at the thought of Ellie leaving. "You're what?"

"A friend of mine from college has a spare room and a job opening at her local diner. I'm leaving tomorrow."

I'm reeling. The last few weeks Ellie's consumed my thoughts. I've allowed myself to think about a future with her in it, and now she's leaving.

"You can't leave." Ellie raises her eyebrows at me completely unaware of what her news is doing to be. "Tell me what happened."

She tells me about overhearing Carolyn and about her stupid high school nick name. By the time she's finished, I'm pacing the kitchen with my hands curled into fists.

"They have no right to speak about you like that."

She's leaning against the counter, and I realize I've been planning our future together but I haven't even told her how I feel.

"I mean it, Ellie. You're ten times the woman that Carolyn is."

She rolls her eyes at me, and I stop pacing and come to stand in front of her. I put one hand on either side of her, trapping her against the counter. "You're smart and you're funny and you're beautiful."

I tilt her head up so she's looking at me. "Those are all qualities that Carolyn doesn't have."

She smiles, and I know I'm getting through. "And you're brave. Brave enough to leave Maple Springs to go away to college, brave enough to enter a five mile race when you've never run before."

"I only did it to impress you," she says with a smile, and my heart jumps. She feels the same way as I do.

"You know what else you have that Carolyn doesn't?"

Her lips are close to mine now, and I can smell the coffee on her breath. She shakes her head.

"Brennan Jacobs as a boyfriend."

She laughs, and I laugh with her even as my heart pounds, wondering if I've presumed too much. But fuck it, her eyes are dancing and she's not pushing me away, so I lean in and kiss her.

A slow sensual kiss, pressing my lips slowly to hers, kissing away all the hurt and pain and letting her know there's someone who loves her. Because yeah, I do love her, just the way she is.

Her arms slip around my neck and she pulls me toward her, and I've never felt so whole, so right.

There's the sound of a door opening. "Oh…"

We break apart to find Ellie's mom staring at us, mouth open.

I glance at my watch. "I, um, better go. I need to get to the starting line."

I dart past Mrs. Smith who's already reaching for the phone. My mom will hear the news before I can get back across the road.

"Wait for me." Ellie calls after me. "I need to get changed. Give me five minutes."

"Are you doing the race?"

"You're damn right I'm doing the race. I'm not going to let Carolyn Summers, or whatever the hell her name is now get the better of me."

"That's my girl." I can't help the grin that spreads across my face as I watch her dash up the stairs.

7

ELLIE

My thighs are burning, and my feet are so heavy that every step is like dragging lead. The road is scattered with empty water bottles and cups as we make the final turn into the park. The clean-up truck is just behind us, sweeping up the debris from the runners.

The old Ellie would have been embarrassed about being just in front of the clean-up truck, but the truth is I really don't care. Because I have run nonstop for almost five miles. I don't care that I'm the last person to come in. I feel like a fucking champion.

"Last half mile around the park," says Brennan.

I nod, because I lost my ability to speak about a mile back. Brennan has stayed by my side the entire way. I tried to get him to go on, but he insisted on running with me.

And I'm thankful for it. He's been my own personal cheerleader giving me words of encouragement the entire way.

We turn into the park, and the final part of the track is lined with people. Even though everyone else has already finished, the crowds are still here. When they see Brennan and me, they go wild.

I can see the finish line now, an archway decorated with balloons.

"Almost there."

I concentrate on putting one foot in front of the other, even though I can't feel my legs anymore.

There's cheering from the crowd, and I hear my name being called. I look up, and Carolyn is smirking at me. "Ellie Elephant."

I stumble and almost trip. Brennan catches me, and I steady myself against him.

"Ignore her and keep going. You're almost there."

But everything has gone hazy, my legs are heavy, and all of a sudden I don't think I can make it.

I scan the crowd, and this time I see Mom sitting with Brennan's mom and brother. They're both waving their hands in the air and cheering wildly.

Next to them are Layla and Lizzie and Penny and

some of the other girls from the businesswomen's network. Penny's just returned from college too and I introduced her to the group.

"You've fucking got this, Ellie!" Yells Lizzie making Carolyn cover her baby's ears and give her a dirty look.

They holler my name and knowing there's all this support in the crowd makes me dig deep and keep going.

"Come on, Ellie." Brennan slips his hand into mine. I stare at him dumbly as he practically pulls me along. "Let's finish this together."

I make myself keep going. Brennan keeps his hand in mine, and the warmth gives me strength.

Then there are figures moving out of the crowd and jogging towards us. I recognize Karl, the old guy, and Gary and Linda, the middle-aged couple, and others from the running club. They're grinning at me, shouting words of encouragement as they fall in with us.

I'm almost at the finish line now, surrounded by my supporters, and as my feet cross the line I'm filled with the most amazing feeling in my heart. Even though I'm out of breath and about to collapse, I let out a massive whoop of joy.

Brennan pulls me into his arms and kisses my

sweaty lips. The crowd goes wild around us, cheering and hollering.

"I knew you could do it," he says.

I've got the biggest grin on my face, and I'm getting slapped on the back by my friends from the running club.

It's the proudest moment of my life, but all I can think about is getting Brennan alone and kissing him again.

BRENNAN

It's an agonizing hour that I have to spend after the race giving out prizes and helping pack up. All I want to do is get Ellie home and make her mine properly.

I keep her by my side, making sure she gets enough to drink and a protein shake. She'll hurt tomorrow, but today she's looking radiant, with her cheeks red and a wide smile, happy at her accomplishment.

Mom rolls by with Ellie's mom. "We're going to have lunch in town. You two want to join us?"

"I need to take a shower," I say quickly. The only thing I want to go is get Ellie alone and claim her as mine.

"And I need a nap," says Ellie. "Maybe another time."

They head off, and as soon as they're out of sight I grab Ellie's hand. "Let's go."

We drive to my place, giggling like naughty school children. "I really need to get my own place," I say, letting us in the front door. "You want a shower?"

She raise her eyebrows at me. "Together?"

"Of course."

Ellie follows me into my bathroom, and I turn on the shower. As steam fills the room, I slide her t-shirt over her head. She's wearing a heavy-duty sports bra with so many straps I don't know where to begin.

She must see my confused expression, because she laughs. "I'll take care of this one."

She wiggles out of the bra while I strip off my t-shirt. I slide down my shorts and briefs, and her eyes go wide when she sees my cock standing to attention.

"Did I do that?"

"Girl, you've been making me hard ever since I saw you walk into that tree a few weeks ago. Now come here."

I slide her shorts and panties down and pull her into the shower. The warm water hits my skin, and as I press my body against hers, I capture her lips in a kiss. I can taste the sweat on her still, salty and tangy.

My mouth moves down to her neck, and she moans as my hands wrap around her body.

"Let me soap you down."

I put some body wash on a sponge and move slowly over her body. The soap suds slide across her skin as I explore every part of her. My dick's hard and dripping with anticipation. I press myself against her, letting the slipperiness of our bodies guide our movements.

"My turn."

She takes the sponge off me and moves it against my chest, leaving foaming soap suds. She works her way down my body, kneeling before me to sponge my thighs.

The sponge moves around to my dick, and I take a sharp intake of breath. Her hand runs down the length of my shaft as the sponge moves over my balls.

"Let me rinse you off."

She puts the sponge down and lets the water run over my dick. Then she leans in, and her lips close around my tip. My eyes roll back in my head, and I lean against the shower wall as her mouth slides down my dick. She licks and sucks as the water falls around us.

My balls are so tight, but I don't want the first time to be like this. It takes all my willpower, but I tilt her head up and slide my dick out of her mouth.

"I want to be inside you."

I pull her to her feet and kiss her hard, tasting myself on her tongue. There's a ledge on the shower that's almost the perfect height, and I gently turn her around so she's bending over it.

I spread her legs and slide against her. She gasps as my dick rubs against her pussy.

"You ready, baby?"

She nods. "Yeah."

I slide my dick into her pink opening, and she pushes back to take me all in. It's tight and wet and feels like home. My hand grabs her ass, and I thrust into her, filling her up.

Her hand moves around to her clit, and as she touches herself, her fingertips brush my balls.

I'm pounding her hard when I feel her tense and cry out. As she comes, I release into her, my load shooting deep inside her convulsing pussy.

It's pure bliss, and in that moment there's nothing else but the two of us.

I pull her to me and hold her tight as the water runs over us.

In my head, I'm already making plans. Moving to our own place and starting a family, because I know without a doubt that Ellie is the only woman I'll ever need. Now that I'm home, I'm staying home.

EPILOGUE

ELLIE

Five years later...

"**M**ommy, Mommy!"

I turn to the voice in the crowd to see my four-year-old jumping up and down excitedly.

"Hey, sweetie!" I detour over to the side of the track and give her a high five as I jog past.

"Almost there!" calls my mom, who's holding the baby. Brennan's mom is with them, and their cheers follow me as I head for the finish line.

Brennan went on ahead, and as I near the finish line, I can see him waving and cheering me on. I glance up at the big digital timer as I cross the line. I'll have to wait for the official timings, but I think I got a personal best.

The Prostate Cancer Foundation charity race that Brennan founded has become a yearly event in Maple Springs. I do it every year, and each year it gets a bit easier.

But mostly I leave the events to Brennan. His special discharge from the army came through so he could take care of his mom and brother.

We moved into our own place just down the road, but we go around every day to help out.

Brennan started a personal training business helping people train for events. He does a lot of triathlons, and we go all around the state while he competes.

I cheer from the sidelines, happy to stick to my once a year five mile race.

He also does some work at the Maple Mountain Veteran's Retreat up in the mountains, that was opened by an ex-military former recluse Sam and his young wife. Brennan helps veterans get back into training with their sometimes life-changing injuries.

Some of the men and women he's worked with are doing the event today. I saw a woman he's working with streak past me on her prosthetic leg.

I'm still one of the slowest in the race, but I don't care. It's not about the speed you do it in, it's about finishing the race.

I took a job with the local council working with troubled children through art therapy. It's part-time, which means I get to hang out with my kids too. The best of both worlds.

Brennan scoops me into a hug and gives me a sloppy kiss. "Well done, girl."

"How did you do?" I ask between catching my breath.

He beams. "Linda got a personal best, and Karl was the first in the over seventies, again."

"Was he the only runner in the over seventies?"

Brennon chuckles. "Yeah, but don't tell him that."

It's typical of Brennan that his success is based on those of his running club.

"There's still a couple more to come in. You want to stick around?"

I remember my first run and how the club came out to run with me for the last quarter mile. "Of course."

Sometimes I have to pinch myself with how lucky I am. At the end of the day, I get to snuggle up to the best looking, funniest, most caring man in the world. I'm one lucky girl!

50

GET YOUR FREE BOOK

Sign up to the Sadie King mailing list for a FREE book!

You'll be the first to hear about exclusive offers, bonus content and all the news from Sadie King.

Allie is a bonus book in the Curvy Girl Can series exclusive to my newsletter subscribers.

To claim your free book visit:
authorsadieking.com/bonus-scenes

BOOKS BY SADIE KING

Maple Springs

Small Town Sisters

Candy's Café

All the Single Dads

Men of Maple Mountain

Curvy Girls Can

The Carter Family

Wild Heart Mountain

Military Heroes

Wild Riders MC

Mountain Heroes

Biker Brothers of Winter Town

Sunset Coast

Sunset Security

Underground Crows MC

Filthy Rich Love

Men of the Sea

For a full list of titles check out the Sadie King website

www.authorsadieking.com

ABOUT THE AUTHOR

Sadie King is a USA Today Best Selling Author of short instalove romance.

She lives in New Zealand with her ex-military husband and raucous young son.

When she's not writing she loves catching waves with her son, running along the beach, and drinking good wine, preferably with a book in hand.

authorsadieking.com

THANK YOU

Thank you for reading my story! If you enjoyed it, please consider leaving a review, they mean so much to authors and it helps other readers find books they might like.

Thank you!
Sadie xx

9 798223 243076